ADVENTURES IN YOUR DREAM: BOOK II OF III

Keeping the Dream

COLORING / WORKBOOK

Written by

JOSEPH CAFFIERO

Illustrated by

LOUISE ROY

ISBN 978-1-7364129-5-4

Introduction

Take the time to **STOP.**
Take the time to **REFLECT.**
Take the time to mindfully **INCORPORATE**
the lessons of *KEEPING THE DREAM.*

The characters in Your Dream are a part of us.
We would like to invite you to welcome them into 'Your Dreams.'

Color the pages.
Find the mixed-up word.
Discover a crossword and do the dot-to dots.
Help Joey figure out a way to get into the balloon basket.
Write about your favorite character
and what you are grateful for.
Feel free to do some or all of the activities,
with or without assistance.

Enjoy adding color, interest and intrigue as you
make this workbook part of the
Adventures in Your Dream experience.

JOSEPH CAFFIERO

Color Joey's name and draw a picture showing him as he joyfully jumps, juggling jacks.

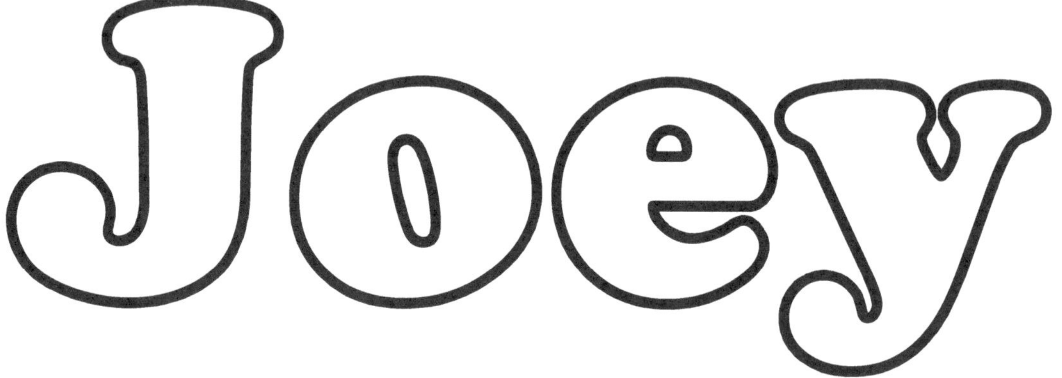

Joey joyfully jumps, juggling jacks.

"I'm supposed to meet Faith in the pasture. Thank you for taking me."

When the webs were done, Joey sat down and began to tie them together with his magic rope.

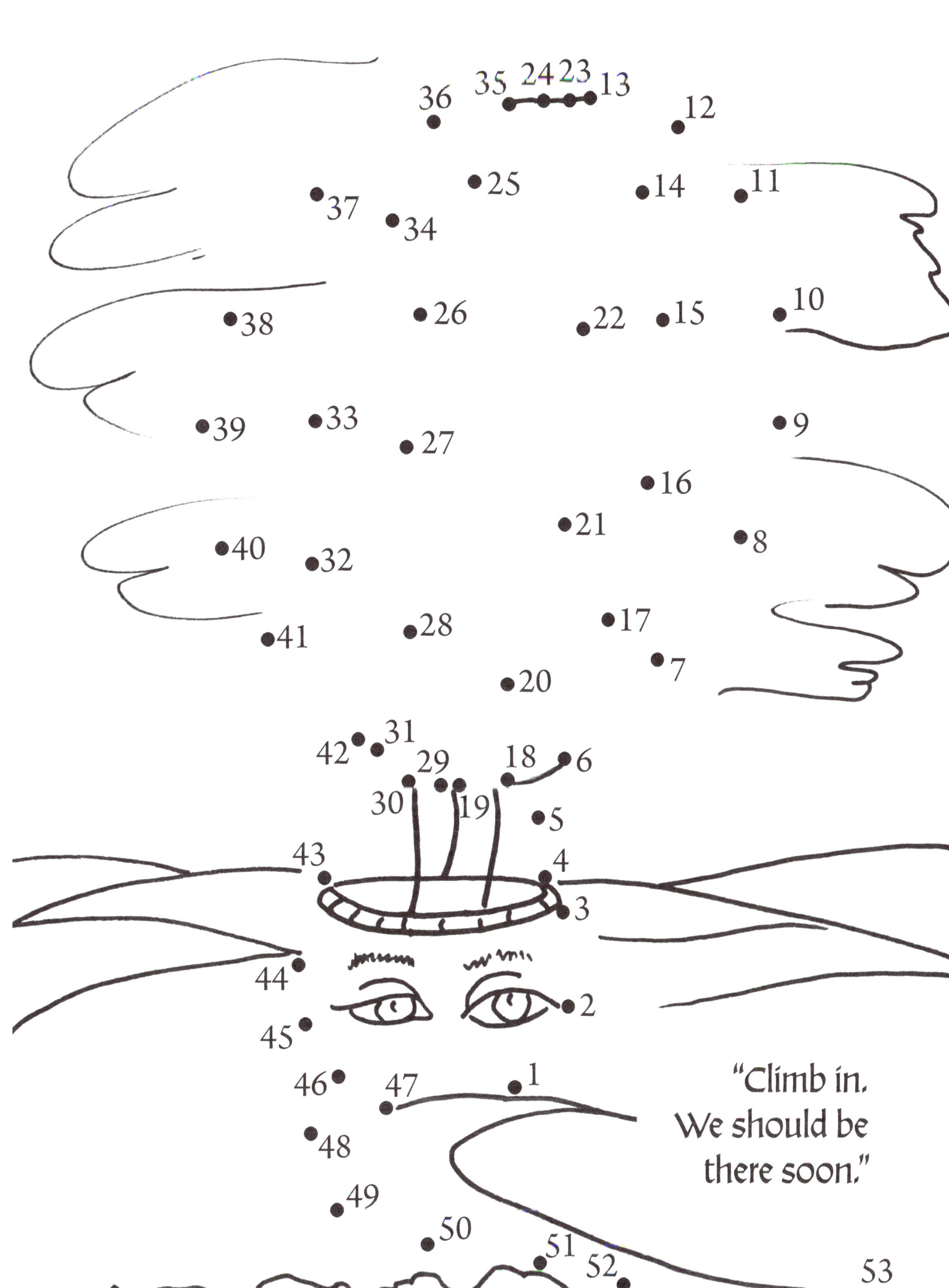
"Climb in.
We should be
there soon."

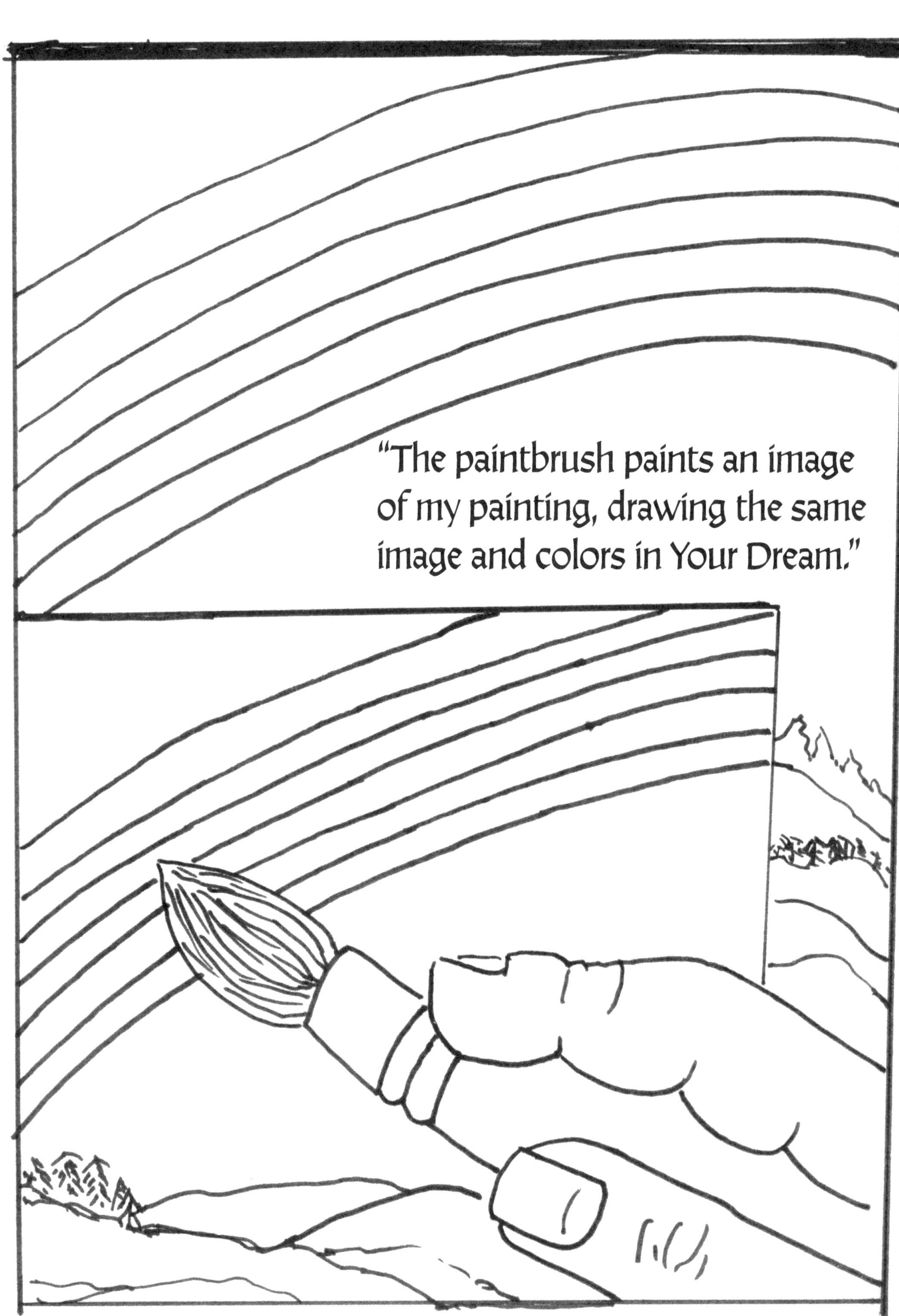
"The paintbrush paints an image of my painting, drawing the same image and colors in Your Dream."

Color Secure's name and draw him as
he sees seaworthy sea serpents swimming south.

Secure sees seaworthy sea serpents swimming south.

The horse gently nudged
his shoulder with his nose.

Color the Goddess's name and draw a picture of her as she gladly grows glistening garden gladiolus.

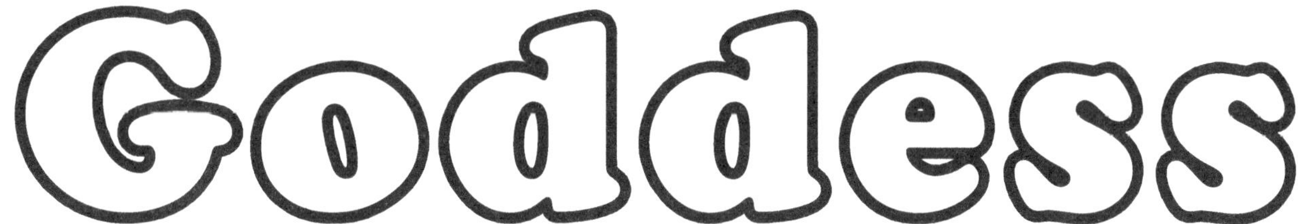

Goddess gladly grows glistening garden gladiolus.

"The Goddess can change her shape as she wishes. Now she chooses to swim with the fishes."

"I will become one of them first," the Goddess said.

The Goddess floated out of the top of the paintbrush.

Color Fire Spirit's name and draw him
as he finds famous friends from faraway farms.

Fire Spirit finds famous friends from faraway farms.

"Look Secure, a wolf is caught in that briar patch!"

Fire Spirit felt
a surge of
confidence
and power fill
his body—
he was their
Alpha leader!

Color Crystal Clear's name and draw
a picture of him as he carefully cuddles cute cubs.

Crystal Clear

Crystal Clear carefully cuddles cute cubs.

"Look Secure, doesn't
that patch of clouds
look like a hand?"

Joey looked up in the sky and waved to Crystal Clear to descend closer to him.

"We will look for her together," replied Crystal Clear. The balloon began to rise.

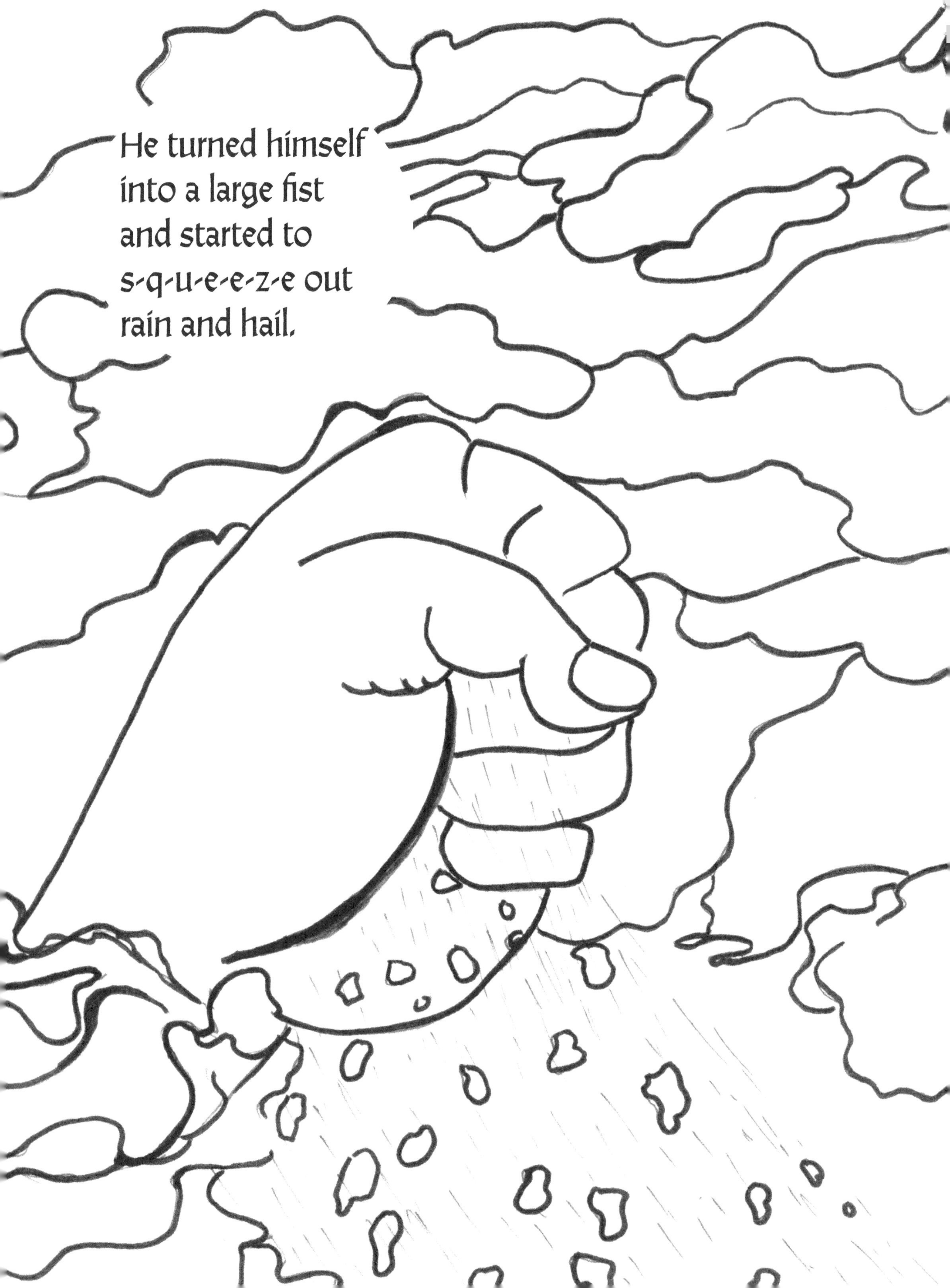

He turned himself
into a large fist
and started to
s-q-u-e-e-z-e out
rain and hail.

Color Dandy Dragon's name and draw a picture of him as he delightfully doodles decorative designs.

Dandy Dragon delightfully doodles decorative designs.

Ferocious led them to a corner of the cave where Dandy Dragon lay curled up into a ball.

"I am adding
smoke to
your rooms.
It will fill you with
dread and gloom."

Color the giant's name and draw a picture of him as he gleefully grows garden grapes gratefully.

Giant gleefully grows garden grapes gratefully.

"The giant was very restless and upset when he was dreaming, until now."

"How is this for teasing
or is it bullying?"

"Sunny Skies, I have never seen such a beautiful crystal from the elves before."

Crossword Puzzle

ACROSS

2. Who had the idea that helped Silly Sheep?
3. Who stole the giant's paintbrush?
4. Who was weak and could not find food?
6. What had a directional antenna and could hum?
8. Who caught a mole "unpainting" sky and flowers?
10. Who makes light by mixing air with chemicals?

DOWN

1. Who made himself into a hot air balloon?
5. Who gave Joey a magical purple headband?
7. Who found the giant?
9. Who went into the mole's hole with Sunny Skies?

WORD BANK

CLUMSY • CRYSTALCLEAR • DANDYDRAGON • FAIRIES • FIREFLIES
FIRESPIRIT • GODDESS • SANDMAN • SILLYSHEEP • SWORD

Color the name fairies and draw a picture of them as they faithfully forage for familiar foods.

Fairies faithfully forage for familiar foods.

After the king's offer, the fairies danced in a circle.

Color Silly Sheep's name and draw a picture of her as she sometimes sadly sits sideways.

Silly Sheep sometimes sadly sits sideways.

"I am st . . . st . . . stuck in this hole," Silly Sheep said.

"Baa, I am scared," Silly Sheep cried. "Do not eat me!"

Color the Myopic Mole's name and color him when he may mindlessly munch moving mites.

Myopic Mole may mindlessly munch moving mites.

The mole is not painting. He …
he … He is 'un-painting.' He is
drawing out the colors in the sky!

"Bathing in rainbow light helps me to feel lighter. My attitude toward living is brighter."

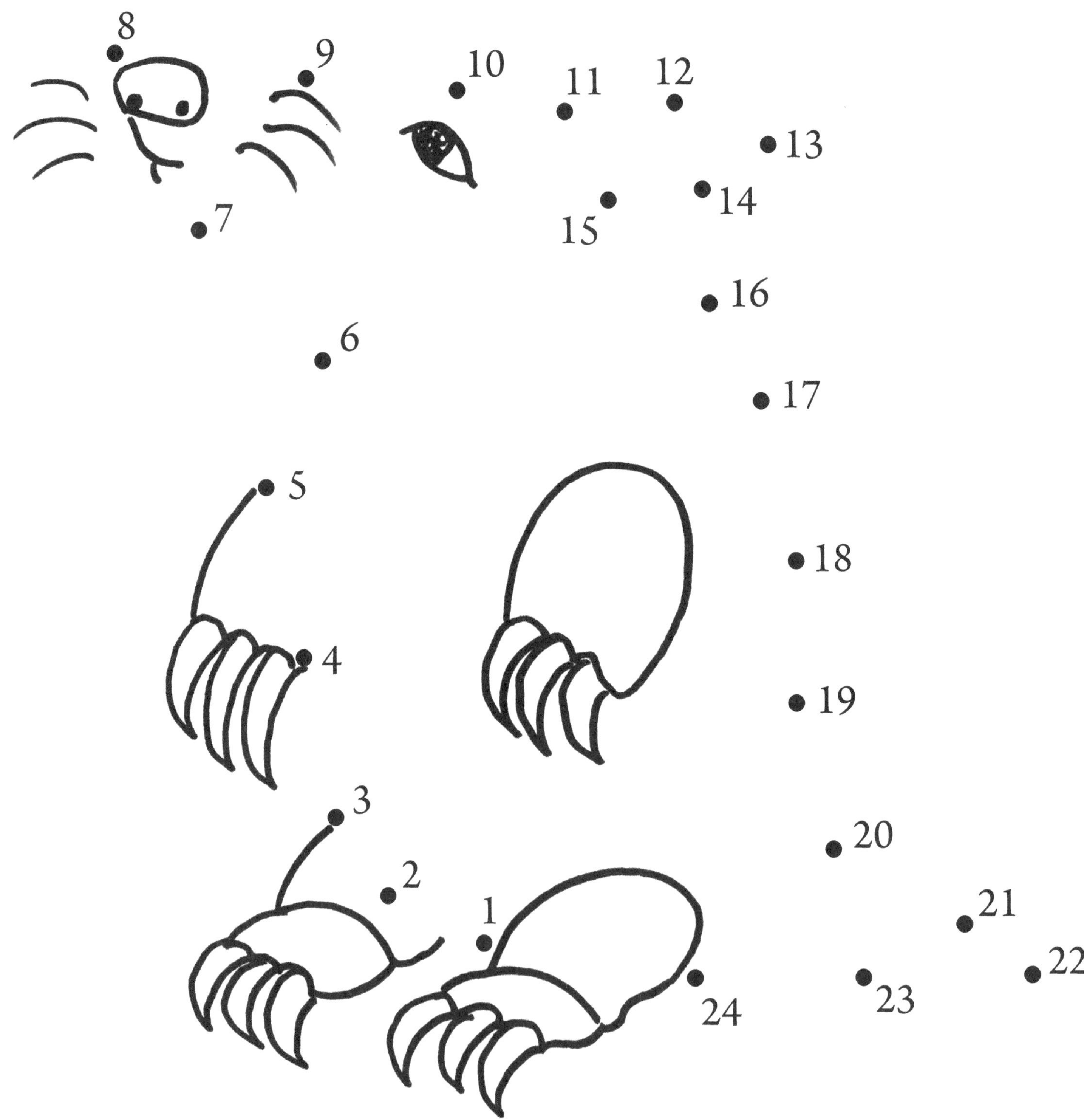

"How nice for
me to move
more easily."

Word Scramble

1. TGNIH ____________________
2. IGREBD ____________________
3. SCRALYT ELACR ____________________
4. EDHR ____________________
5. SNMID ____________________
6. EOHP ____________________
7. DRVOCEYSI ____________________
8. LEROEPX ____________________
9. IINEGNBNG ____________________
10. GDSDEOS ____________________
11. ERTWEAH ____________________
12. CEESRU ____________________
13. REFI IPSIRT ____________________
14. KINFE ____________________
15. BKKCPCAA ____________________
16. IATHF ____________________
17. DEANHDAB ____________________
18. NNUIOMTA ____________________
19. SWVEOL ____________________
20. TAME ____________________

WORD BANK

backpack • minds • meat • Secure • explore • hope • beginning • Night
Faith • Fire Spirit • Herd • headband • Goddess • discovery • wolves
Crsystal Clear • mountain • weather • knife • Bridge

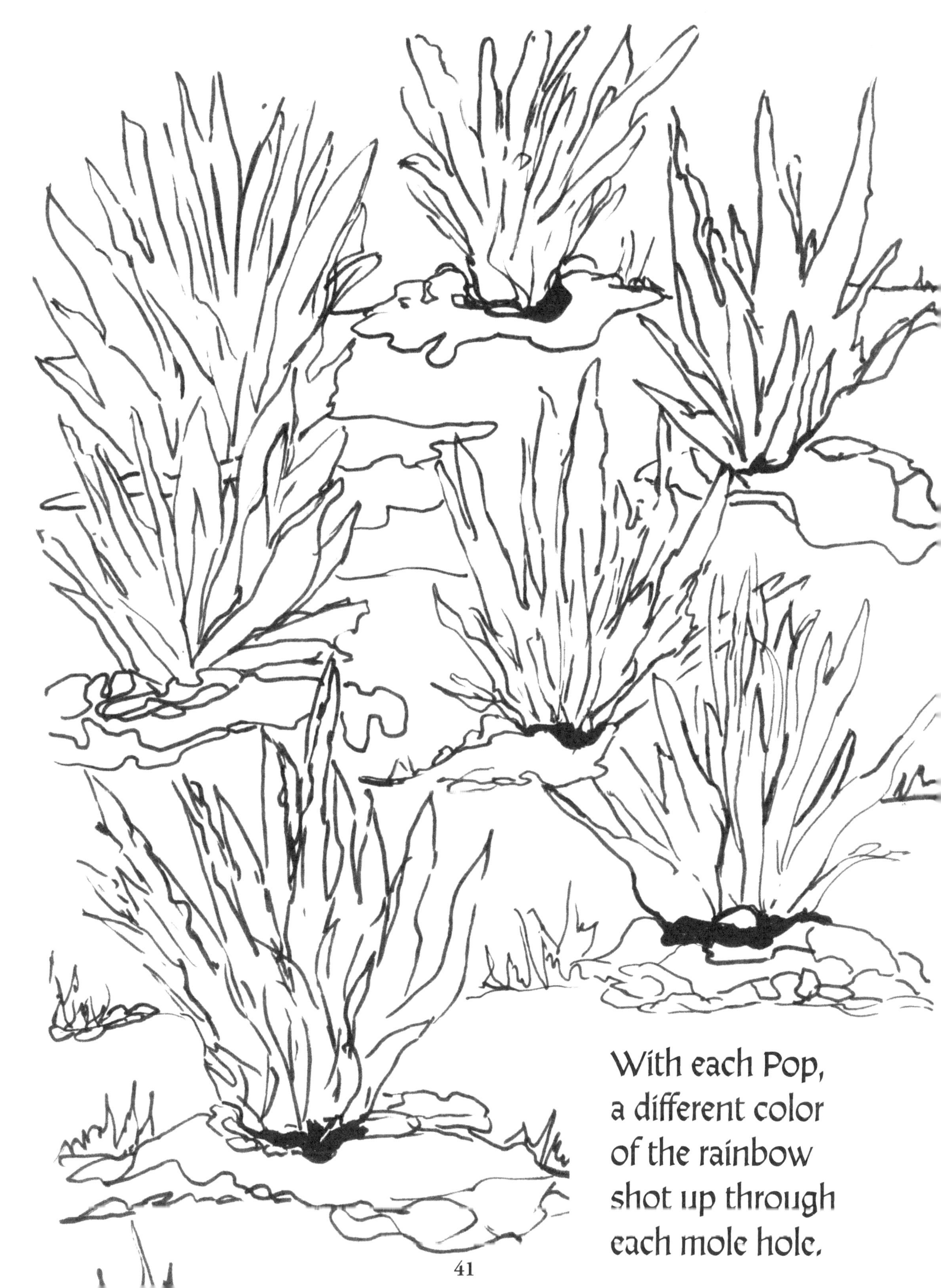

With each Pop,
a different color
of the rainbow
shot up through
each mole hole.

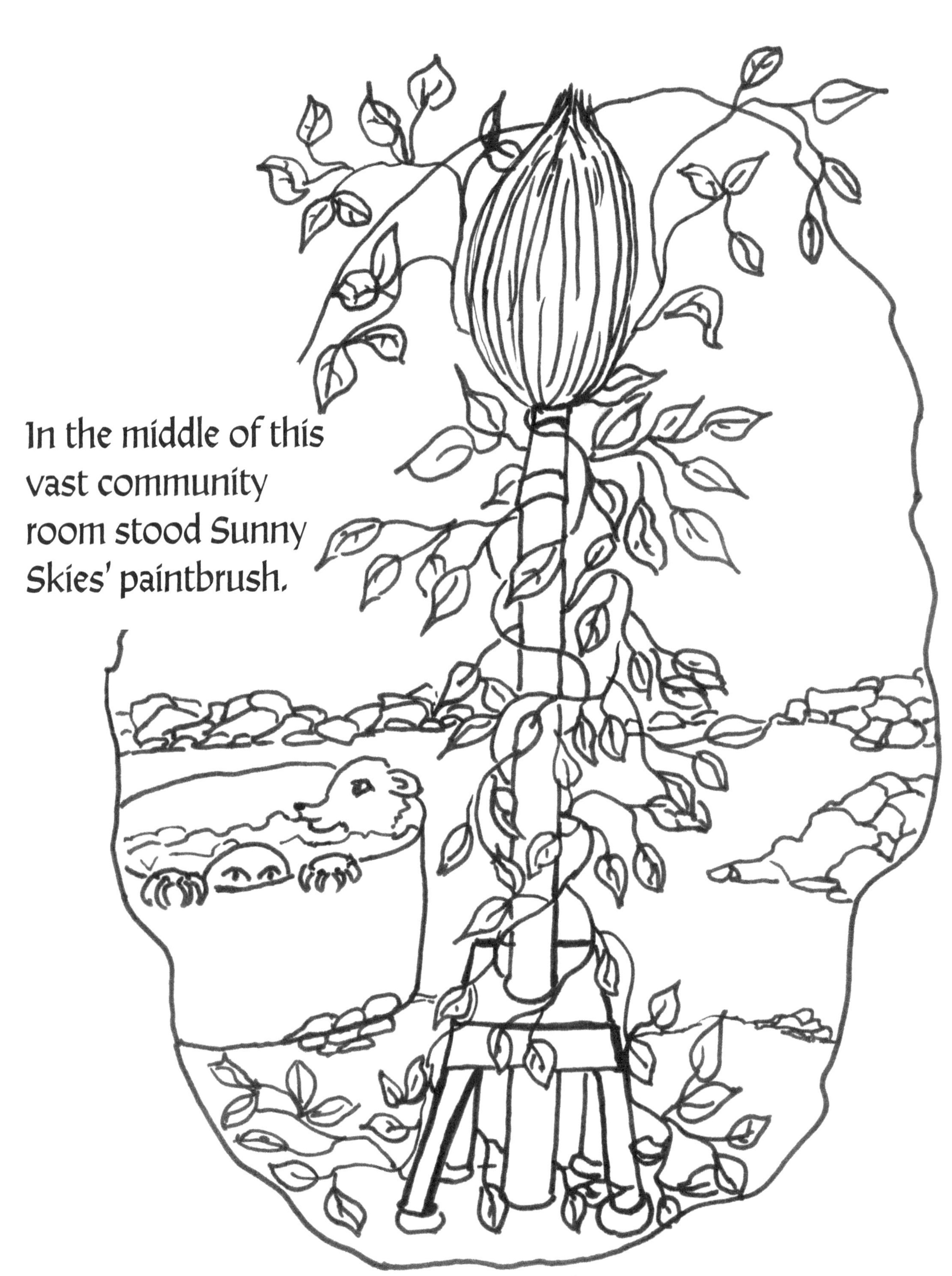
In the middle of this
vast community
room stood Sunny
Skies' paintbrush.

As Secure trotted away from the rainbow bridge, he turned around to take a last look at the rainbow colors.

"This cloud will always have an open heart and a silver lining because of you."

Write about what you would want to say to your favorite character in KEEPING THE DREAM.

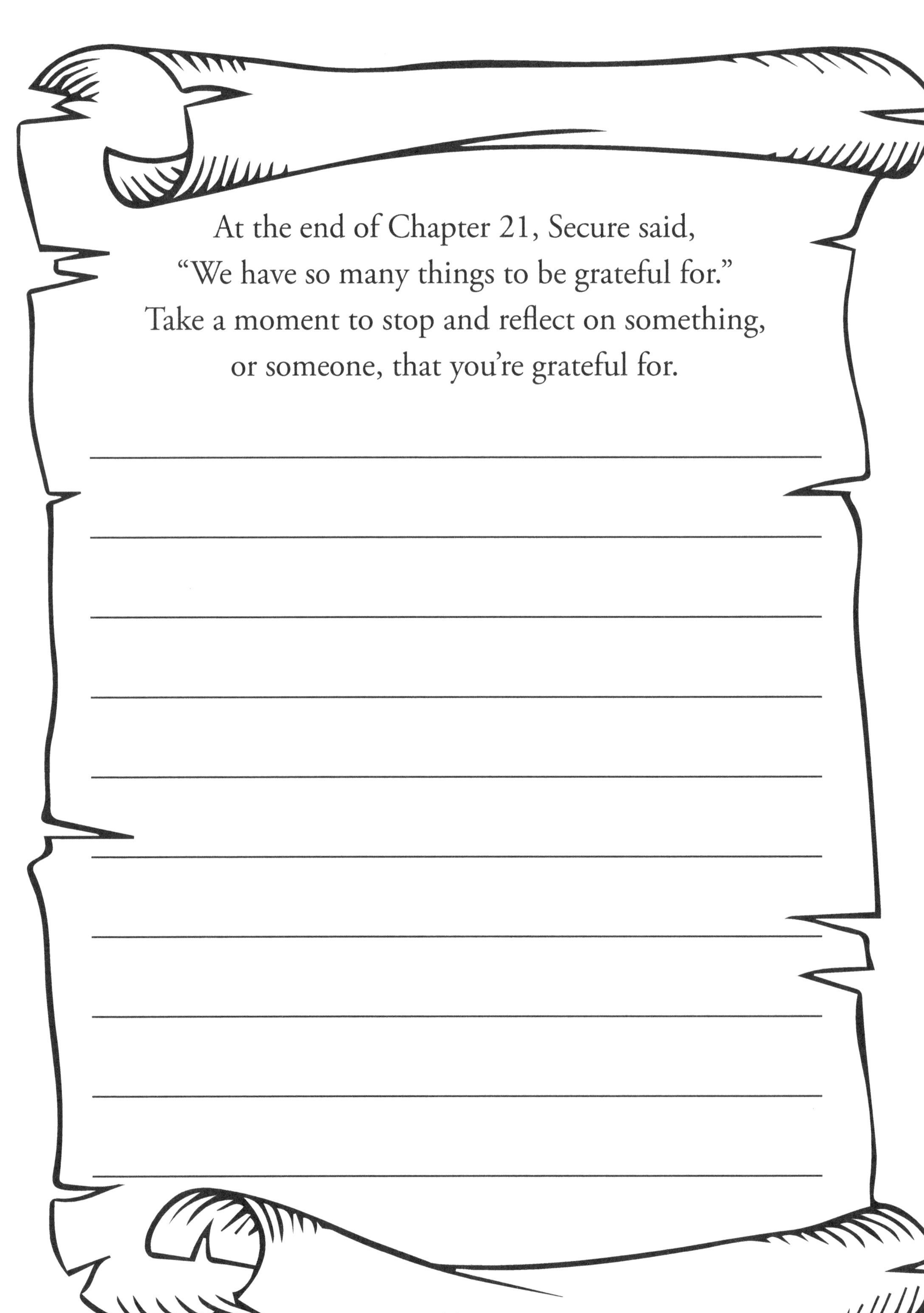

At the end of Chapter 21, Secure said, "We have so many things to be grateful for." Take a moment to stop and reflect on something, or someone, that you're grateful for.

Word Scramble

In the book, *Keeping the Dream*, Joey teaches the animals in Your Dream to meditate with mindfulness. Can you make twenty words or more, using the letters in **m-i-n-d-f-u-l-n-e-s-s?** The first one is done for you.

1. in ____________________ 11. ____________________

2. ____________________ 12. ____________________

3. ____________________ 13. ____________________

4. ____________________ 14. ____________________

5. ____________________ 15. ____________________

6. ____________________ 16. ____________________

7. ____________________ 17. ____________________

8. ____________________ 18. ____________________

9. ____________________ 19. ____________________

10. ____________________ 20. ____________________

Trilogy Summaries

There are three books in the saga of ADVENTURES IN YOUR DREAM.

BOOK I, THE DREAM, finds the protagonist getting ready to go to elementary school. He has a hard time dealing with bullies. Joey has adventures and meets Guides in the realm of Your Dream, that teach him to do mindfulness meditation. He uses this knowledge to gain confidence and deal with bullies. Joey learns to tame his own inner dragon.

BOOK II, KEEPING THE DREAM, has the protagonist in middle school. He is asked to help the Guides find out who or what is taking the color, sound and Life Force out of Your Dream? Bullies try to thwart his endeavors. He leads mindfulness meditation to find solutions to these problems.

BOOK III, LIVING THE DREAM, has the protagonist in high school. He can no longer travel into Your Dream—the portal is closed. Joey learns a new way to access his Guides. Using mindfulness meditation and other tools he learned in Your Dream, he finds the courage and inspiration to redirect bullies and help rebuild his school and community.

Special thanks to the illustrator, Louise Roy,
whose artwork brought *Keeping the Dream* to fruition.

www.ingramcontent.com/pod-product-compliance
Lightning Source LLC
LaVergne TN
LVHW082221181224
799472LV00039B/1772